D1525360

Starry Night

Not All Who Wander Are Lost

D.P. Conway

Part of

The Christmas Collection

Day Lights Publishing House, Inc.

Cleveland, Ohio

From Darkness to Light through the Power of Story

The Christmas Collection

Read in any order.

Dedications

To Marisa
In Honor of Your Brother

For my biggest fans,
Colleen, Bridget, Patrick, and Christopher

And for my littlest fans,
My little Aubrey and my little Avery

Chapter 1

"Wake up, young man."

I heard a faint voice, and as it faded into nothing, a gentle breeze cascaded across my face, and my mind began to stir.

Had I been sleeping?

Was I dreaming?

The scent of wet grass filled my nostrils and instinctively, I inhaled, conscious of my breathing for the first time. It felt good to feel my chest rise and fall, drawing in the fresh air.

My eyes were tired, closed tight, too heavy to open.

The voice came again.

"Young man, wake up."

Who is calling me?

Realizing I was not dreaming, I drew in another breath, and slowly opened my eyes.

The stars in the sky and the cloud of my own breath shimmering and floating upwards in the moonlight told me it was night.

The voice came again, asking, "Are you alright?"

The dark shape of a man was standing, hovering over me.

His voice was low, and deep, and laced with a steady gentleness I was not used to hearing.

I squinted, looking more closely. He was of average height, husky, and holding a long staff in his hand. Behind him, hanging low in the sky, was a full moon, shining its light brightly onto the top of the cloth turban, wrapped tightly around his head.

"Who are you?" I asked.

"I am Jesse," he responded. He slowly extended his hand to help me up. His face was illuminated by the moonlight, and I felt the kindness emanating from his large eyes and subtle warm smile.

Somehow, I knew I could trust him.

Somehow, I knew that he wished me no harm.

I took hold of his outstretched hand and clasped it. His hands were strong and rugged, not the hands I was used to shaking. As I sat up, I put my own hands to the ground to support me and immediately felt the soft, slightly damp grass. I looked all around.

I was in a vast, rolling field.

In the distant moonlight, were the outlines of hills, cascading up and down across the endless horizon.

The man did not ask me any questions. He seemed to be giving me a moment to orient myself. My eyes were adjusting to the night, and I looked up at him again. He stepped to the side and now the moonlight illuminated his body entirely. He was dressed in a way I had never seen anyone dressed before.

His turban was burgundy colored, and partially hung down his back. He wore a thick brown shirt that stopped just above his knees and was tied at the waist with a thick leather belt. His pants were cream-colored, plain and baggy, and tucked into thick fur socks that rose high above his ankles. On his large feet were sturdy leather shoes with slight openings on top that made them look like some sort of sandal.

He resembled a strong warrior, and yet at the same time, he resembled a gentle shepherd.

He was both at once.

"Where am I?" I asked as I looked around, shivering, for the first time noticing the chill in the night air.

He answered in a calm, comforting tone, "You are in the hill country."

"The hill country?" I said as I glanced around again, trying to see beyond the dark slopes of the horizon, but there was nothing to see in any direction except the dim outlines of distant hills.

I asked, "But… how did I get here?"

"I don't know," he replied. Then his voice grew more somber as he said, "I was going to ask you the same thing."

I sat still, trying to remember something, anything. I did not know how I had gotten there. I could not remember, and yet I knew I should have an answer. I looked up at him, feeling foolish, and hoping he might see my sincerity in not answering.

His face was strong, with a set jawline, covered by a rugged beard. His dark eyes stared down at me as if he were penetrating my thoughts. His thick eyebrows were narrowed and though very still, revealed a growing understanding. He was wondering about something, and as he did, a brief look of concern crossed over his face.

I began to mumble, trying to find words that would not come. My heart raced, and I nervously spilled out unintelligible mutterings, trying to force my words to remember for me, trying to say something, but nothing would come.

I lowered my eyes from his, ashamed, unsure what to say or do. I could not remember anything at all.

I looked back up.

A warm smile had settled on his face, and he nodded.

He somehow… understood.

Somehow… he trusted me.

Out of the corner of my eye, something moved, and I turned my head. There was a shadowy mass in the not-too-distant field. I looked closer and realized that it was a flock of sheep. Hundreds of them were sitting still in the cool night air.

I now heard their faint, gentle bleating.

The entire scene looked surreal to me, the sight of a flock of sheep sitting under the light of a full moon. I wanted to capture the scene, never to forget how special it looked.

Then, something else moved.

There were other men, a small number of them, perhaps five or six, walking nearby the flock, each man holding a long staff, each man dressed like Jesse. They were walking around the perimeter of the flock, periodically bending down and petting their sheep.

I turned to Jesse and asked, "Are you, shepherds?"

"Yes, we are," he said, smiling. "Here, let me help you up."

He reached down, and I extended my hand again and this time he pulled me up.

I winced, "Ahhh!"

"What's wrong?" he asked, as now the other shepherds looked over to see what was going on.

"I don't know?" I said, worried, as I placed my hand on the back of my leg just above my knee. Pain shot through my leg again as my fingers ran through a thick, warm, partially dried substance on my leg. It felt like blood. I pulled my hand into the moonlight, confirming my suspicion. "I'm bleeding."

"Let me see," Jesse said. He placed his strong hand on my shoulder, steadying me, bent down, and examined the wound. "Hmmm, yes," he said, "you have a bad wound. We will need to clean and bandage it."

Jesse started to turn toward the other shepherds, but then stopped, and turned back with a concerned look on his face, He asked, "Do you know how this happened?"

"No, I don't remember," I said, as I tried to take a step but stopped, wincing in pain again.

"Sit back down here," Jesse said, grasping my hand, and easing me back to the ground. He said, "I will have my men get the needed supplies."

He called out to the others, "Bring water, rags, and herbs."

At once, two of the shepherds left the flock and headed away quickly. The rest started walking toward us, gathering around one by one, looking down, curious as to who I was.

"Who is he, Jesse?" one asked in a gruff voice.

Jesse turned to him, his face bearing a half-smile, and shrugged, saying, "I don't know yet."

All of them took his answer in with caution. Their faces, made clear by the moonlight, showed their collective concern as to who I was and why I was suddenly in their midst. There was a warmth in their concerned looks, a gentleness, but one born of strength and confidence.

They looked as though they had faced trouble before.

They were not afraid.

A few sheep began to wander nearer to us, wanting to be close to their shepherds. They were bleating softly, as one might imagine they would do at night when they were apart from the flock. I could smell their coats and their unmistakable earthy animal scent. It did not bother me, though, as I thought it might.

It smelled ancient, it smelled of the land, and of the old ways I remembered hearing about during my life.

'My life.' The phrase struck me as odd.

Yes, I had a life. Of course, I did. But I could not remember it, and yet… I remembered hearing things, like the 'old days,' but from whom?

What old days?

Jesse interrupted my thoughts as if he had known them. "Where are you from?"

"I don't know.… I just woke up here."

The gathered men's collective faces glanced to one another, not bearing ill will, but rather, a tinge of concern.

Jesse knelt down on the grass next to me, "What is your name?"

I shook my head, feeling embarrassed, and replied, "I… I… don't' know my name."

Jesse looked up into each of the others' faces as if he were collecting their unspoken responses. He sighed, as a man would who knew he had a difficult task ahead of him. He then patted me gently on the shoulder, saying, "Don't worry. It will come to you."

The two shepherds came running from the back of the flock with the supplies. They knelt next to me, saying nothing, but went right to work, cutting away the back of my pant leg and skillfully cleaning my wound.

It hurt tremendously, and I grimaced and winced, trying not to cry out, feeling as though in front of these strong men, I would appear to be weak.

The men who were gathered around watching, were very quiet. One wandered away back to the flock, but the rest stayed, watching. Those attending to me used a damp rag and did a final rough cleaning of the area. They applied the herbs, packing them down against the wound. They held them in place and carefully bandaged me with a long cloth, wrapping it uncomfortably tight around the whole of my right thigh.

When they finished, they gathered their bandages and herbs and went back in the direction from which they came, disappearing into the distance.

I sat up, wincing slightly.

Jesse handed me a flask that had been hanging around his neck. "Here. Take a sip of this. It will help you."

As I drank the cold water from it, he reached into a pouch hanging down from his other shoulder and pulled out a piece of bread. He handed it to me, saying, "Eat this."

The bread was a little stiff, but I was so hungry that I savored every bite, and for the first time, I realized I had not eaten in a long time. Then suddenly my mind flashed back, only for a moment. I was holding a fresh piece of bread, looking up, saying something to someone, and then, as quickly as I remembered this, the vision faded.

Who had I been talking to?

Jesse watched me eat the piece of bread, then handed me a wineskin, saying, "Wash it down with a sip of wine, but not too much. Too much is not good for you right now."

The crisp grape flavored wine gently took the remaining morsels of bread down my throat. The wine was more refreshing than I ever remembered drinking. It left my thirst feeling quenched, completely satisfied. I handed the wineskin back and said, "Thank you, Jesse."

Jesse reaffixed the wineskin over his shoulder, and said, "I am afraid you will have to stay with us for a while. That leg will take time to heal. Get some rest now. Tomorrow will be a long day. We will make our way to a new pasture."

"Thank you," I said as I nodded, still confused. But the idea of resting sounded too good to question.

One of the shepherds came over and handed me a wool blanket. As I laid there, I watched the rest of the shepherds walk away, some bedding down nearby, others farther out by their sheep. Then, slowly, all grew quiet.

For a moment, my mind flashed back again, I was in a home, with others, and yet I was somehow alone. I could not see who they were. Their faces were not visible.. Then, as fast as it had come to me, the flashback was gone.

I laid awake for a long time, trying to remember more, watching the moon set and the stars move across the sky, listening to the occasional bleating of the sheep.

I wondered about the shepherds, about me, about not knowing who I was.

Finally, I succumbed to the timeless bandit of sleep.

Chapter 2

The following morning, I stirred, awakened by the noise of sheep bleating very loudly. I sat up, rubbing the sleep out of my eyes. The sun was well up, its warm light shining on a lush green pasture filled with hundreds of sheep, all milling about aimlessly within the confines of the flock.

It was as if they were saying good morning to each other, careful not to miss anyone. There was an excitement in their cries that I had never heard before in animals.

The shepherds, seven of them in all including Jesse, were walking among them, checking on them, apparently preparing for the day's journey. Jesse looked over at me and waved. He shouted a few instructions to the others, then walked over. "Good morning, young man. Did you sleep well?" he said, in a boisterous voice.

"Yes, I did,"

I tried to get up, but I winced in pain and carefully eased back down onto the grass.

"Easy now," Jesse remarked, "that leg needs time."

He moved next to me and helped me to stand, then handed me his staff. "Walk with this today and stay close to me. We are going to be moving the flock to a new pasture a few miles over in that direction." He pointed to a distant hill.

I looked out at the hill, feeling a sudden surge of adventure I had not known in as long as I could remember. Somehow, I realized that in my life I had longed for adventure, and never been able to have it. I replied heartily, "I would like that."

"Good," he said with a reassuring smile.

He started to turn, then stopped and turned back, saying, "By the way, I'm going to call you Marco."

"Marco," I chuckled, "Why Marco?"

"After Marco Polo, the famous traveler. I can see you are a traveler."

His words struck me, and I remarked, "Marco Polo, yes, I have heard that name."

"Well, that is your name for now," Jesse said.

He walked away, and I began to smile. Marco. I liked the sound of this name and the feeling of adventure that was surging within me matched it perfectly.

~ ~ ~ ~

We spent the day moving the flock of sheep along the terrain, across large fields. We walked for miles, up and down rolling hills, each one leading to a crest that revealed even more hills in the distance.   Though it was not easy for me because of my wound, the day was very peaceful. I never remembered working as hard or walking as far. The whole day was one of teamwork. The shepherds, though seemingly working apart, were actually working closely together as one unit, guarding the sheep, going after the strays, keeping them moving toward the new distant pasture Jesse had told me about.

The sun began its descent early that day, and I realized that we must be in the late Fall or Winter season of wherever we were.

When dusk finally came, the flock was slowed and brought to a stop. They were grouped together closely. I watched the shepherds busy moving among them, putting them down for the night. Before long, the noisy bleating of them all quieted down. A calming, brought on by the setting sun seemed to embrace us all, man and beast alike.

The shepherds gathered together not too far a distance from the front of the flock. A neatly organized small camp was effortlessly set up.

In the center of the camp, two of the shepherds built a fire and placed a grate over it using strong sticks, They laid modest amounts of deer meat on top of it, and waited for the flames to grow larger.

The camp was arranged in a large circle and held no tents, but rather, just spots along the outer perimeter where each shepherd unfurled a woolen blanket designating where he would sleep. The men opened and emptied their satchels reorganizing them as they put order into their space. I had nothing to organize, but Jesse showed me a spot to use for my own bedding, and I spread out the blanket I had rolled up earlier and carried on my back during the day.

Soon, it was dark, and the fire roared to life, and the deer meat cooked quickly. There was enough for each man to have several pieces. Small chunks of bread and greens and berries the men had collected earlier in the day were distributed.

We sat on the ground in a circle around the fire, eating quietly, talking very little. It was as if they were letting the day's long journey ease into the past. When we finished eating, the conversations and interactions increased, with all seven of the shepherds taking turns telling stories, laughing, chiding each other playfully, and periodically passing around a wineskin to help warm their bones.

I did not say much at all, preferring to listen. I still had no memories, but I felt uneasy as I realized that I had no such stories. I had never experienced such camaraderie as these men easily did, but the very fabric of my being seemed to relish it and yearn for more.

As the night wore on, I gathered my courage, and asked, "Where are you all from?"

All grew quiet, and the eyes of all the men turned to Jesse, signaling that he was the one to answer. Jesse paused, staring into the fire, and said, "We are from a distant land, Marco." He looked up and pointed at a star high in the sky. "See the North Star there."

I looked up, "Yes, I see it." It was the brightest star I had ever seen, shining high in the sky, like a lone sentinel watching over the universe.

Jesse pointed in the direction from where we had come, saying, "Once you see that star, Marco, look due west. There, on the far western edge of the hill country is where our homes lie. It is where our families are waiting for us to return."

I looked into the distance, knowing wherever he pointed was too far to possibly see, but it was reassuring to know where they were from and that they had families waiting for them. I realized I must have a family too, somewhere, but where? In what direction?

Jesse continued, "We are called the Shepherds of the Night. Every year, at the end of Summer, we gather our flocks and follow the stars along an ancient path. Then, after the Fall season, in the early days of the Winter season, we finish our journey and bring our flocks to the market. We then return home and spend the Spring and Summer with our wives and families. The following year, we do it all over again."

"That sounds amazing," I said. I asked, "What do you mean, follow the stars?"

Jesse nodded and looked out into the distant sky. "Well, Marco, at the end of summer, certain stars become visible. It is our signal to begin our journey and we follow them until the Great Star appears."

"The Great Star?"

Jesse nodded, "You will see it, Marco. It will become visible in another month or so. The appearance of the Great Star marks a milestone in our journey. It is just after seeing it that we will go to the market and then turn and begin our journey home."

Home.

The words tried to break through the fog in my mind. I tried to see something, anything, but no image came into view. Sadness descended within me, and I understood it was connected to home.

I asked, "Jesse, do you think that I will still be with you then?"

"Yes. I am afraid that you will probably be with us for the whole journey. The nearest towns are more than a week's journey away, too far and too dangerous for anyone to go alone."

"I see," I said, pondering his words. All I could do was trust him.

Jesse watched my reaction and said, "It looks like we are going to have to make a shepherd out of you."

I don't know why, but I liked that. It brought me a sense of comfort. I replied, "I would like that very much."

Jesse perked up, "What do you think, men? Does Marco have what it takes to be a Shepherd of the Night?"

One of the shepherds replied, "I think he does, Jesse."

The others nodded in agreement, some saying 'aye.'

It was silent for a moment as I stoked the dwindling fire with a stick. "What does it take?" I asked, now growing curious at the prospect.

Jesse smiled at the other men, then looked at me, "It takes something special, Marco, more than herding sheep. You have to be chosen to be a Shepherd of the Night. You have to show that you are worthy. We shall see how things work out."

I knew not to say anything else. All that had been said was for my hearing, and it was all that was to be told to me as of now.

We enjoyed the fire a while longer until finally, one by one, they all went off to sleep. I got under a blanket and laid awake for a time, thinking. I felt at home with these men, and I could not remember ever feeling that way in my former life.

Chapter 3

For the next month, I worked alongside the men, learning their ways. We were shepherds by day, moving our flocks, and by night we camped, told stories, laughed, and enjoyed each other's company. It was the most marvelous and most fulfilling time I had ever experienced, and yet, I did not know how I knew this. Part of me felt afraid, uneasy, as if I did not deserve to feel this way or was not capable of feeling such deep down happiness.

It made me want to remember even more who I was in my past life. Every day and every night, I wondered and fought to remember. My questions to myself were ever-present, and yet, being on this journey gave me an overwhelming feeling of peace I had never known, and one which I was becoming increasingly aware I would not want to give up.

One night, after the fire dwindled, and we were about to turn in, Jesse came over to me. "Marco, tomorrow night, the Great Star is due to appear. In the morning, very early, we are heading to the edge of the Great Forest, where we always camp on the night it arrives."

My eyes widened with excitement. I had been thinking about this Great Star since the first night I had been told about it. Now, with the mentioning of the Great Forest, my fascination grew. It seemed we were heading to a magical place. I replied, "I'm looking forward to it, Jesse."

Jesse's smile widened further, "It is a special star, Marco. It is a special night."

"Why is it so special?" I asked.

"You will see, Marco. You will see."

The following morning, we set out with a new resolve. Everyone was pushing hard, driving the sheep forward, keeping a good pace, as all knew we had an important date with destiny.

By late afternoon, as the sun began to set, we crested a hill, and suddenly the Great Forest came into view.

I stopped, as did the other men, all of us allowing the sheep to crest the hill by themselves and head down the opposite side. We stood on top of the hill, marveling at the breathtaking sight in front of us.

The Great Forest spanned the vast horizon, its trees stood like sentinels forming a great impenetrable wall. Its trees were tall, straight, dark green pines. There were thousands upon thousands of them, one next to the other, and as many behind, filling the visible landscape. It was no telling from here how dense it was, but it was wider than any forest I had ever seen.

We continued onward.

The day passed quickly as the ever-present forest grew nearer and nearer. Near sunset, we crested the last hill, and suddenly the forest was within reach, only a short distance away. We set up our camp a few hundred yards from the edge of the tree line. We built a large fire and sat down to enjoy our dinners.

As dusk descended, the sky grew purplish red, giving all a deep sense of peace. Then, the night came upon us, and we all waited.

There was little talking during the rest of the night. All were in thought, staring into the fire, with preoccupied looks on their faces. A calming quiet hung over us, a welcoming silence. The sheep were unusually silent, too, as if they were also expecting something special to arrive.

The night air grew crisp, and a hush fell over the fields, like one I had never known. The quiet of this night had its own energy. It was indeed a special night, just like Jesse had said it would be.

I glanced over at Jesse. He was staring peacefully into the fire, mesmerized in thought, periodically glancing up to the distant night sky.

I was glad he had found me.

Spending time alongside him was silently teaching me things, things I could not quite put my finger on.

It had changed me.

It was as if there was an intrinsic transferring of his demeanor, and his ways into the depths of my thirsting soul.

Suddenly Jesse's eyes widened, and he pointed, exclaiming, "There it is!"

Chapter 4

Jesse and all the shepherds turned to look to the east. A bright star appeared, seemingly out of nowhere, hanging low in the sky as if it were the moon.

But it wasn't the moon.

The sight of the star, majestically beaming through the crisp cold night air mesmerized me.

All the shepherd's eyes were fixed upon it, warmly marveling at it, their faces bearing looks of deep content as if a long-lost friend had just come in from the cold bearing news of good tidings.

As we watched, another light appeared, much smaller than the Great Star. It drifted in toward us from the sky above the distant dark field, drawing ever closer. Without saying a word, Jesse and a few of the shepherds stood, and slowly left our camp, and began walking toward the approaching light.

The light continued moving toward them.

Then, it stopped.

The light seemed to take the shape of a woman, with long flowing blonde hair. She was beautiful to behold, and dressed in a shimmering white dress, whose train flowed magically in the sky behind her. Something was protruding from each side of her back. It took a moment for me to see they were majestic white wings, and I suddenly realized that she was an Angel.

The Angel stopped about twenty feet in the air above Jesse and the shepherds. Her warm smile beckoned to them. They bowed reverently and looked up with their arms outstretched. They appeared to be listening to a message. I realized that an exchange was taking place, but not one of words, as no one was speaking. It seemed rather to be an exchange of thought, transmitted by light.

No sooner had the light appeared than it vanished, and the beautiful Angel was gone.

Jesse and the others turned and walked back to us, and I sensed that the magic of the night was following along with him. He was bringing a message from the Angel.

He said, "Everyone, gather together. There is news. There is a lost sheep. We need to find it. All of you spread out." He paused, nodding, and said, "You know what to do."

He then turned to me, "Marco, you are to come with me."

All at once, everyone moved in unison as if they had been expecting this news. I had no time to think as Jesse brushed past me, saying, "Follow me, Marco."

He quickly walked away from our campfire, across the brightly lit field, and toward the edge of the Great Forest. As we got closer to the tree line, its actual size became apparent. Tall, majestic pine trees, taller than I had ever remembered seeing, towered up hundreds of feet over our heads.

I peered into the forest, but all I could see was the depths of a darkness, darker than I had ever seen.

Jesse went to the edge of the tree line and turned, saying in a calm, but authoritative tone, "Stay very close to me, Marco. You do not want to lose your way."

A tinge of fear shot through my veins. I remembered facing darkness like this before, not so very long ago, but where, or exactly when, I could not remember. But I remembered feeling fear then too, as I had gone into that darkness. I felt Jesse's eyes measuring me, and the feeling of fear, the fear of getting lost in the darkness again held me frozen in my tracks.

Jesse stepped into the woods, turning slightly, motioning for me to follow. He was almost all the way in, and there was no time for me to hesitate. I forced myself to step forward quickly, and ran up behind him, following him in.

The forest was very dark with faint glimmers of moonlight shining through, barely allowing me to make out Jesse's staff and shadow directly in front of me.

"Jesse I can't see," I exclaimed, trembling, afraid I would surely lose him as soon as we went further into the density.

"Don't worry, Marco" he said, "Just stay close to me. I know the way through."

I stayed right with him as we quickly marched through the darkness, zig zagging our way around trees, stepping over fallen logs, brushing back branches, ducking our way along. We were treading on what felt like a path laden with a thick blanket of soft pine needles. My breathing quickened and I began to feel anxious as the darkness deepened, and now, it felt like we had been in there for a very long time.

My mind flashed back to the darkness of another kind, on another day, not long ago, when I was alone, in a place not unlike this, and I had been very afraid. I had blacked out. I remembered now. I had blacked out in that darkness.

"Marco!" Jesse's voice snapped, calling me out of my thoughts. "Hurry, we are almost there."

I had fallen behind.

I quickened my pace, closing the gap between us, frantically brushing beyond branches in my way. I caught sight of him and drew close again.

Suddenly, a light appeared. In the distance, there was a break in the trees.

A clearing was coming into view.

My heart raced with gratitude.

We had made it through.

Moments later, we stepped out of the Great Forest and walked into the dark cold night and onto an immense snow-covered field.

Chapter 5

As we stepped into the field, the air was colder and crisper than when we entered the forest. It was still night but the sky was darker on this side of the forest, though I could still see the Great Star as if it had followed us. At the far end of the field, there were a few people gathered around a fire.

Exasperated by the tension of being so long in the dark woods, I stopped and asked, "Jesse, where are we going?"

"We are looking for the lost sheep." He said as he glanced over at the men around the fire in the distance, studying them, trying to determine who they were. He turned and looked at me with resolute eyes, saying, "I know those men. They may know something. Come with me."

We walked across the field, our feet lightly crunching on the thin layer of freshly frozen snow. As we neared, I counted three men, all older than Jesse. Each of them had a neatly trimmed beard. They wore long colorful robes, with colorful cloth turbans wrapped around their heads, similar to, but more elaborate than Jesse's head covering.

As we stepped into their camp, the three men all looked up, their faces warm and friendly. One of them raised his hand in a welcoming gesture.

Jesse bowed low, and rose slowly, saying, "Greetings to you good men of old."

One of the men replied, "Greetings to you, Jesse. Who have you brought with you?"

"This is Marco," he said, gesturing toward me.

The men's glances turned to me, but they said nothing. Standing before them gave me a deep sense of peace. I was in the presence of greatness, and kindness, and goodness. I had seen them before, I was sure, but how? Where? By their richly colored clothing, I got the sense they were wealthy, but what were they doing here by this fire in this snow-covered field? And how did they know Jesse?

For a few moments, all three of the older men casually studied me up and down, but mainly they looked into my eyes, as if they were measuring me by them. Then, almost at once, they all nodded subtly with a silent, welcoming, gesture of approval.

One of them said, "I am Caspar, this is Melchior and Balthasar. Welcome, Marco."

"Thank you," I said, trying to remember where I had seen them.

The one called Balthasar turned his glance to Jesse and asked, "What brings you here on this holy night, Jesse?"

Jesse paused, as if participating in some ancient ritual, He glanced up at the Great Star for a moment, his eyes sparkling with hope, then looked back at Balthasar and said, "I have been sent this night to look for a lost sheep. Can you help us?"

Balthasar nodded, and his eyes momentarily closed. With eyes still closed, he stayed perfectly still, as if he was summoning some inner power. The others lowered their glance, honoring his silence.

Then, Balthasar nodded subtly, as if a revelation had come to him, and with a confident look on his face, he opened his eyes and lifted his hand into the night air.

He said, "Behold." His eyes drifted and he pointed beyond us, causing us all to turn.

In the distance, a quaint snow-covered valley appeared, with over a hundred homes lining several blocks. They were modern homes, with warm lights aglow inside, and many of them adorned with Christmas lights and wreaths on the outside.

I had a weird feeling, almost like a memory, that somehow, I had seen the place, or perhaps a place like it before. I turned to Jesse, excitement building, and said, "I think I have seen this place before."

Jesse put his hand on my shoulder and turned to face the three men, still sitting in their robes around the fire. Jesse bowed low, then rose slowly as he had the first time, and said, "Thank you, good men, of ages past. I will see you again, with God's help."

None of the three replied, except with their eyes. Their eyes spoke to us, warmly and full of mystery, their faces bearing profound happiness, a happiness that seemed to belong to the ages.

Chapter 6

Jesse and I walked away, crossing the frozen field, and went down the grassy, snow-covered hillside that led into the valley of homes below.

Near the bottom of the hill, our feet stepped onto a snow-covered street, and all became more vivid. The noise of festivities in many of the houses could now be heard. From the houses, a warm glow was felt all the way into the street where we were walking. As we turned onto the main street in the development, snow began to fall. We turned down a quieter side street with nearly ten homes on each side, all adorned with glowing outside Christmas lights.

Everything was silent now, except for our footsteps softly crunching the fresh layer of snow. As I walked in the middle of this quiet street, I sensed I had somehow been here before. Even the wind chilling my bones was familiar to me, but I had no context for ever having felt it. This was somehow connected to the life I had been searching for, but I could not break through to the memories I so desperately sought. I closed my eyes and I tried to remember but it was to no avail.

A tear fell down my cheek.

Then, all at once, a memory shot through my mind.

Home.

Yes, that feeling of home I had brushed upon over the past months, unable to place, resurfaced.

I stopped in my tracks and turned to look at one of the houses. "Jesse," I said, "that one over there. I have been in that house."

Jesse looked over, his brow furrowed, studying it carefully. He said, "We may stop there for a moment and see why you recognize it, but we must move on after that. We must keep looking for the lost sheep."

"OK," I said, feeling a sense of trepidation. There was something about the house that caused me to feel tense. Perhaps Jesse was right. We would stop only for a moment, then move on.

He led the way toward the place I had pointed to, and I followed. We walked up the car-lined driveway to the front porch. It was a modern Colonial-style home, made of sand-colored bricks. Two large picture windows looked out to the street from either side of the large maroon door. A large green wreath, adorned with red and gold ribbons hung prominently in the center of the door.

We walked next to the window on the right and peered through the frosted glass. A family was gathered around the fire. I immediately recognized a woman inside. She had dark brown eyes and thick dark hair—I knew what her voice would sound like just by looking at her, and yet, I still did not know her name.

The interior and the furnishings were even more familiar. I had definitely seen them before. I had been inside this house.

I looked at Jesse, and I nodded, signifying we had the right house. He waved his staff in the air, and suddenly we were inside, standing near the front door.

Inside, felt beautiful, warm, and familiar. The festive decorations, Christmas table settings, and lit candles were also distinctly familiar. I was drawn to look at the woman with the dark eyes again. She was the woman I had seen glimpses of over the past few months.

All at once I realized who she was.

It was my older sister, Marisa.

She had been like a second mother to me during my life.

It then came to me.

It was Christmas Eve, and we were at her house. It was where we had always gathered on that night.

The house was crowded with people that I began to recognize. My mother was there, and my two brothers, and some of my cousins. Many of my nieces and nephews were there too.

I knew them all yet; still, I did not know who I was.

Jesse stood next to me perfectly still, not saying anything, but allowing me to think.

I began to grow anxious, just as I had felt standing before the dark forest. My heart grew heavy, as I feared I might never know who I was.

Chapter 7

As Jesse and I stood by the door, unnoticed by anyone, my sister Marisa called for everyone to gather around the dining room table.

Jesse looked over at me, his eyes seeing if I wanted to go closer, but I shook my head. I wanted to stay right where we were at.

Everyone moved into the large dining room and sat around the large cherry wood dining room table. It was filled with dishes of meats, potatoes, rolls, and vegetables. A large Christmas centerpiece of flowers adorned the middle of the table.

Marisa stood up at the head of the table. She bowed her head for a moment, then said, "Welcome, everyone. As you know, it is a sad time for us this Christmas because we lost our dear brother this year."

She paused, letting her words settle on the quiet guests before continuing, "I wanted to take a moment to remember him." She bowed her head, as did the others.

She continued, and began choking up, "He had a very hard life and… I just hope he is happy now. I miss him terribly." She wiped some tears from her eyes, as her husband came over and put his arm around her.

All around the table, everyone's heads were bowed in somber silence. I swallowed, and a sinking feeling fell upon me. Was she was talking about me? *Lost our dear brother? Yes, I… I was lost.* But… were they talking about me?

They finished their moment of silence.

It was still quiet, as Marisa sat down and began passing the plates of warm foods around. Gradually, the noise and the laughter and the talking that accompanies large family gatherings commenced. I marveled at the beauty of the organized chaos that I had never before noticed to be beautiful, which now I could see plainly as an outsider, looking in.

At one point, my sister got up and walked away from the table, holding back tears. She walked over to the fireplace and looked up at a picture on the mantel. I looked to Jesse who nodded, then walked across the living room and stood behind her, getting a closer look at what she was staring at. I don't know how I knew, but I knew it was a picture of me standing next to my deceased father. She stood there for a long while, looking at the picture of my deceased father and me, not saying a word. I moved next to her so I could see her face. I wanted to hug her, but somehow, I couldn't.

She closed her eyes and whispered a prayer. I watched her lips move gracefully and felt honored she was remembering me. A tear emerged from her eye and rolled down her cheek. I reached out my hand and gently caught it.

And suddenly, I remembered who I was.

I turned to Jesse and exclaimed, "Jesse, I know who I am now. I know what happened." My mouth opened wide, and a shiver ran down my spine, and I froze. My excitement gave way to a growing sense of dread, my hands went cold, as I looked down at them, turning them over and back. My eyes began to water. "Jesse, I died... just a few months ago... it was... unexpected."

Jesse nodded, his face bearing the strength he wanted to give me but knew I alone would have to summon.

I looked again at the picture on the mantel, and said the words I knew to be true, "My name is Ernest."

Jesse nodded with a concerned look. He was observing me, as a caretaker would observe one under his care. I looked back at everyone in the room, as a feeling of despair began to descend upon me.

I had thought once I knew who I was, I would no longer feel lost, but now that I knew who I was, I felt more lost than ever.

Though I was home, I did not feel at home, and then I remembered my life.

I turned to Jesse and started talking out loud, as quickly as I could, as the memories rushed back, "Jesse, I... I never fit in. My life here... it was so hard... I struggled with so much. No ever one understood me."

A tear rolled down my cheek, and I looked around the room. "Jesse, being around my family was very hard for me... I did not like myself at all. I had so many problems, and... I felt ashamed of so many things... like I was a failure in life... especially near the end."

Jesse put his hand on my shoulder, "But Ernest, these people loved you."

"I know that they did... but it didn't help me. I mean... even though I knew they loved me... I still felt like I was a burden to them."

I wiped another tear off my cheek.

Jesse nodded as if he understood and said, "Let us stay a while longer, Ernest."

We walked over by the fireplace. Jesse studied the picture of my father and me. His brow furrowed some, as if he were trying to understand something. I was curious why he looked at the picture so long.

I turned away and watched my family eating and talking at the table. I was happy that they were happy, and yet...

how could I be happy. I wanted to fit in. I wanted to like who I was... and now... and now... it would never be. My life was over.

It was too late to ever love myself.

I was gone.

I looked at Jesse and saw the sadness in his eyes. He was somehow reading me, understanding me.

We stood together in silence, watching them all. After a little while, I said in a somber voice, "I want to go now."

Jesse nodded and walked to the front door. I followed him out, turning one more time to look back at my sister.

She had been like a mother to me. She loved me unconditionally and understood me like no one else.

I did not know if I would ever see her again.

I would miss her, but I could not stay.

It was all too late.

Chapter 8

Jesse and I walked outside, down the car filled driveway and back onto the snow-covered street, following the now faded footprints that had led us there. We trekked back up the hillside and out of the valley, and back across the snow filled field. The men were still sitting by the fire. They waved to us, then resumed talking with each other. The Great Star still hung in the sky, but it was more distant now, its light having faded some.

We headed back toward the edge of the mysterious Great Forest, then stepped into the trees and began the journey home. All seemed much darker. I was no longer afraid of losing Jesse, no longer afraid of falling behind, no longer afraid of the darkness.

The journey through was longer this time, and much harder. Earlier, though I had felt fear at times, the joy and urgency of finding the lost sheep had spurred us on. Now, there was no reason to hurry. I felt empty.

There was nothing to look forward to, and for me, it felt like there was nowhere to go.

We lost our brother this year.

Yes, I was as lost as I had ever been.

I was walking through a dark forest that was darker than I had ever seen. I felt like laying down and staying there. Tears began to softly fall down my cheeks, but I welcomed them.

They were all I had.

I looked ahead. Jesse had his head down as he walked. He too, felt the heaviness I did. He really cared about me. He had been a good friend to me. I would miss him too.

But where would I go. I did not know, but more than anything, I needed to be alone, like I had always needed to be alone. Like I had always been alone.

Perhaps, this was my destiny.

Perhaps, this was my end.

I looked up as the darkness gave way and a clearing came into view, and we stepped out of the Great Forest.

Something was different.

It took me a moment to realize it, as I had been lost in thought, but we came out of the forest in a different place from where we started.

The Great Star was there, though, nearer now, and still shining brightly on the landscape below, lighting it as if it were a bright full moon. Across the field, in the distance, there was a large, long, single-story home, made of white stone, with a thick thatched roof. Smoke was billowing out of the chimney.

"Where are we?" I asked Jesse.

"It is the home of some friends of mine, Ernest. We will stop and get something to eat before continuing back to meet up with the others. Tomorrow, we will start for the market."

I sighed. Nothing would ever give me joy again. I was sure of it.

We walked up to the house. Next to it was a smaller structure that looked like a barn. I peered into the open barn windows. It was dark inside. Outside, though, were several horses, all with saddles on them. The horses were standing perfectly still. The breath from their nostrils rose into the cold night air, turning to a cloudy mist. Their brown coats glistened in the light of the ever-present Great Star.

We walked over to the home with the thatched roof. Inside I could see a warm fire glowing. Many people were gathered inside the house, but there were no modern Christmas lights, as the other home had, just candles and a large fire.

We went to the large wooden door in the front and Jesse knocked. The door opened slowly. A woman with shoulder-length brown hair and brown eyes stood before us. She wore a simple brown tunic, half-covered by a blue kitchen apron, Her eyes beamed when she saw Jesse. In an Italian accent, she said heartily, "Hello, Jesse, come in. We thought you might not come tonight."

Jesse's smile grew wider than I had ever seen, "Hello, Rosa. I have brought someone with me. Do you mind?"

"Someone with you," she asked as her eyes narrowed. She looked at me curiously, measuring my eyes as the three older men around the fire had.

She asked, "What is your name?"

"Ernest," I said.

She looked me up and down for another moment, as if trying to decide, then relaxed and smiled, "Come in, Ernest. You are welcome here, this night."

She warmly took my hand and ushered me into the home. I walked into a bustling scene of men and women, all dressed in plain clothing, as if they lived in another century. They were talking happily, smiling with each other, and laughing.

Candles adorned the tables and walls, and a roaring fire blazed at the far end in a magnificent stone fireplace, perfectly warming the large room.

Suddenly I heard a loud booming voice from across the room, "Ernest!"

My eyes widened.

The voice sounded very familiar.

I looked across the room to see who it was. It was my dad who had died many years earlier. He was beaming, hustling across the room, dodging his way through all the people to get to me. He was younger than I ever remembered, his head full of shiny black hair I only recognized from pictures.

He thrust himself forward and embraced me. "Ernest, we have found you."

"Dad, where am I?"

He turned to the crowd with tears forming in his eyes, "Everyone, Ernest is here! We have found him!"

I looked around, confused, knowing that there was something I had not fully realized yet. I asked, "Who are these people?"

"Look closely, Ernest," my father said, "It's your family and many of our friends."

I quickly turned to look back at the woman who had opened the door, and I suddenly recognized her, but she was young too, and different "Grandma?" I asked.

She too, was beaming with joy. "Welcome home, Ernest." She warmly hugged me.

The rest of the family came over. Uncles, aunts, and members of my family, friends too, from long ago that I remembered as a small child, all gathered around me.

One by one, I recognized them as they hugged me and re-introduced themselves to me, all glad to see me.

I suddenly realized that I was home.

I would be welcome here.

I was one of them, and for some reason, I no longer felt troubled. I no longer felt alone.

It was more than that, though. I was no longer ashamed.

Working with Jesse and the other shepherds had helped me to like myself again.

Amidst the chaos, I turned to tell Jesse something and he was gone. I quickly went across the room looking for him, and saw him walking toward the door. "Jesse," I called out as I ran over to him. "Jesse, wait. Do you have to leave?"

He smiled and said, "Yes, Ernest. I still have work to do this night."

I asked, "Will I see you again?"

"Yes," he said, looking down, thinking. Then he looked up and said, "at the end of Summer, I will come for you."

"You will?"

"Yes," he said, "I want you to journey with us next year."

"Really?"

"Yes, I want you to help us to find lost sheep."

My heart leapt inside me. I said, "You mean, become one of the Shepherds of the Night?"

"Yes," he said, as a small smile formed on his face.

I asked, "But do I have what it takes?"

There was a long pause, then a large smile drifted onto his face and his eyes gave me their reassuring look. "Yes, you have a big heart, Ernest, and that is what it takes."

I smiled, wiping a tear from my eye.

I understood.

"Goodbye, Ernest," Jesse said.

He turned, opened the door to the night air, then stopped, and turned back, saying, "Ernest, there is one more thing."

"What is it?" I asked.

"Merry Christmas," he said, smiling.

I heartily replied, "Yes, Merry Christmas, Jesse."

He waved, and then he left.

Suddenly someone inside broke out in song, and all chimed, in, heartily singing, "God rest ye Merry Gentlemen, let nothing you dismay. Remember, Christ, our Savior, was born upon this day. To save us all from Satan's power, as we had gone astray. Ohhh, Tidings of Comfort and Joy, Comfort and Joy. Ohhh, Tidings of Comfort and Joy."

The end? No, it is only the beginning.

Dedicated to our dear brother, Ernesto, who struggled all his life, and who we lost three months before Christmas in 2018.

You will always be in our hearts, Ernesto.

Until we meet again.

The Story of the Writing of Starry Night.

A year after the death of my brother-in-law, I had been thinking for some time of writing a story about a person like him, but I never had the idea. I had also been thinking of writing a Christmas story. Then, a few days before Christmas, I decided to read a classic story to my grown children on Christmas Eve, as I used to read to my children in the evenings when they were young.

I searched all the classics and could not find one I thought they would enjoy. So, I decided to write my own, and Starry Night was born. It was a labor of love and done in a few days.

It was written to honor my wife's deceased brother and inspire my children and family with a heartfelt Christmas story that captured the unique and singular magic that descends upon us all, the world over, once a year. It is a magic we have all known and felt. It is the magic of that one night, when Heaven comes down to Earth. It is the magic that is Christmas Eve.

D.P. Conway

Final Things

Could you rate this book with on Amazon?

Review on Amazon

To find me on amazon, search DP Conway books.

Sign Up for my Monthly Newsletter at

dpconway.com

I promise not to annoy you.

Drawing from his Irish American heritage, D.P. Conway weaves faith and hope into his storytelling, exploring the profound mysteries of life and its connection to the Angels, the Trinity, and the rest of the unseen Eternal world we are all part of. (…world without end. Amen)

His works consistently convey the triumph of light over darkness, inspiring readers to find strength and solace amidst life's trials.

Also by D. P. Conway

Stand Alone Novels

Las Vegas Down

Parkland

The Wancheen

Marisella

The Christmas Collection

Starry Night

The Ghost of Christmas to Come

Nava

Twelve Days

Home for Christmas

Coming Soon

Mary Queen of Hearts

And hopefully many, many, more....

Afterlife Chronicles: Angel Sagas Series

The Epic Series based on Genesis and Revelation

Dawn of Days

Rebellion

Judgment

Empire

The Innocents

And 7 more titles in this epic series.

See many more of D.P. Conway's books on Amazon

or visit www.dpconway.com

Copyright & Publication

Daylights Publishing
5498 Dorothy Drive Suite 3:16
Cleveland, OH 44070

www.dpconway.com
www.daylightspublishing.com

Photo sources and credits are listed at www.dpconway.com

Cover: Colleen Conway Cooper
Developmental Editor: Colleen Conway Cooper
Final Developmental Editor: Carolyn Knecht
Copy Editor: Connie Swenson

Made in the USA
Columbia, SC
05 March 2024

32727963R00036